JUST BRASS

directed by

Philip Jones and Elgar Howarth

TROMBONE SOLOS

VOLUME ONE

arranged and edited by
JOHN IVESON

CONTENTS

CHESTER MUSIC

TROMBONE SOLOS
1.
THE EARL OF SALISBURY'S PAVANNE

arranged and edited by
John Iveson

William Byrd

CH55320

1

2.
VARIATIONS ON
THE ASH GROVE

Traditional

3.
I ATTEMPT FROM LOVE'S SICKNESS

from *The Indian Queen*

Henry Purcell

4.
SKYE BOAT SONG

Traditional

5.
LO SEE THE CONQUERING HERO

George Frederick Handel

6.
LONDONDERRY AIR

Dreamily ♩=60

Traditional

7.
WALTZ
Op.39 no 15

Johannes Brahms

8.
AN ENGLISH MEDLEY

COME LASSES AND LADS

LAVENDER'S BLUE

BRITISH GRENADIERS

18

10/00 (38361)